MARVEL

The AVENGERS
EARTH'S MIGHTIEST HEROES!

HULK™
VERSUS THE WORLD

ADAPTED BY
Elizabeth Rudnick

STORY BY
Christopher Yost & Joshua Fine

WRITTEN BY
Brandon Auman

EXECUTIVE PRODUCERS
Alan Fine, Eric S. Rollman, Dan Buckley, Simon Phillips

DIRECTED BY
Vinton Heuck

3 1389 02114 3805

MARVEL
NEW YORK

© 2011 Marvel Entertainment, LLC

Marvel, The Avengers, Hulk, and all related characters and the distinctive likenesses thereof are trademarks of Marvel Entertainment, LLC and all its subsidiaries, and are used with permission. Copyright © 2011 Marvel Entertainment, LLC and its subsidiaries. Licensed by Marvel Characters B.V. www.marvel.com. All rights reserved.

Published by Marvel Press, an imprint of Disney Book Group. No part of this book may be reproduced or transmitted in any form or by any means, electronic or mechanical, including photocopying, recording, or by any information storage and retrieval system, without written permission from the publisher. For information address Marvel Press, 114 Fifth Avenue, New York, New York 10011-5690.

Printed in the United States of America

First Edition
1 3 5 7 9 10 8 6 4 2
J689-1817-1-11121

ISBN 978-1-4231-4558-5

www.marvel.com

The Las Vegas Strip was packed with tourists. Among the crowds walked a lone man. This was Bruce Banner, otherwise known as the Incredible Hulk.

Suddenly, a police car squealed to a stop. The cop chased Bruce, and he took off running. Bruce got away once again. . . .

Meanwhile, inside his tank, General Ross was determined to capture the Hulk once and for all.

The general wanted answers. And he knew once he locked up the Hulk, he would get all he needed.

Bruce was also looking for someone. He entered a diner and looked around. A very large man was sitting at the counter sipping soup. Bruce took a seat next to him.

"Carl 'Crusher' Creel?" Banner asked. The man ignored him. "I've been trying to find you for weeks . . . and I know S.H.I.E.L.D. is looking for you, too. I'm here to help you."

"How'd you find me when S.H.I.E.L.D. couldn't?" Crusher asked in a deep, rumbly voice.

It was a good question. "Because you're emitting gamma radiation, Mr. Creel," Bruce answered. "You could say I'm an expert on the subject."

Crusher, like Banner, had been exposed to radiation. Crusher had been taken to the Cube, a Super-Villain prison where monsters were created from men. There, he'd become the Absorbing Man.

"I'm afraid S.H.I.E.L.D. is trying to turn prisoners into weapons," Banner said.

Absorbing Man smiled evilly. "It's funny. You never asked me how I escaped," he said, holding up his spoon. He stood up and absorbed the metal from the utensil. His whole body turned into solid silver!

Then, with one shove, he sent Bruce flying out of the diner.

"I've been looking forward to a fight," the big man said and followed him outside.

In seconds, Bruce Banner transformed from a mild-mannered man into the Incredible Hulk! Towering over the Absorbing Man, he let out a ferocious ROAR!

The fight was on!

The battle raged as the two giant monsters fought, leaping off mountains and hitting each other with large metal signs. The Hulk hit the Absorbing Man very hard, but all he did was make a tiny dent!

BANG! CLANG! CLONG! The two monsters continued to fight.

Hulk was just about to put an end to the Absorbing Man when a missile suddenly hit him! General Ross and his men had arrived.

Huge tanks, whirring helicopters, and armored vehicles charged in Hulk's direction. **"All Hulk-buster units open fire!"** Ross ordered.

Hulk batted away the missiles as if they were baseballs. Then he leaped high into the air and ripped a rocket launcher off a copter. Now **HE** had a weapon. He began firing back!

Suddenly, over the tank radio, a voice said, "General Ross, withdraw your men. Now!"

It was S.H.I.E.L.D. agents Black Widow and
Hawkeye! They had come to take the Hulk to the Cube.
Hawkeye fired several kinds of arrows at the Hulk.
One carried a net and another a shock of electricity.
One even trapped the big, green monster in a block of
ice! After a long battle, the Hulk was down.

Suddenly, a missile streaked through the sky— right for Hawkeye and Black Widow! The Incredible Hulk jumped straight at the missile, smashing it out of the sky. The Hulk had saved Black Widow and Hawkeye! But he had been knocked out by the blast and was now going to be taken to the Cube as a prisoner.

Later, Hawkeye visited Banner in his cell.
S.H.I.E.L.D. had always told him the Hulk was a monster.
But Hawkeye witnessed him be a hero. That was not
the act of a monster. And now, the giant bound before
him was just . . . a man.

"**Maybe the question** you should be asking is what S.H.I.E.L.D. wants the Hulk for," Bruce said, as if aware of Hawkeye's hesitation.

Banner nodded at the room around him. "Do you really think the Cube is a **JAIL?** They have samples of my blood." He paused. "They want to make more of me. . . ."

As Hawkeye left the cell, he saw Black Widow
entering a lab—where the blood samples were kept.
Why would she be going in there? he thought.
Suddenly, he remembered Banner's words. Hawkeye
had a terrible feeling.

He quickly went to the computer to look up all the communications and field reports by Black Widow.

"Files are not located on the network," the computer said. "Communication records were transferred to a remote computer."

Hawkeye didn't like the sound of that. He hacked into Black Widow's records and played a recent report.

"S.H.I.E.L.D. suspects nothing," Black Widow said to someone Hawkeye couldn't see. "I'll retrieve the sample."

Hawkeye's heart began to race. Who was his partner talking to? He checked the video display and gasped.

She was talking to a HYDRA agent!

There was no time to lose. Hawkeye followed Black Widow into the desert and watched as she walked up to several HYDRA agents, the canister containing the Hulk's blood sample in her hand.

She was about to hand it over when—**WHACK!**—One of Hawkeye's arrows knocked the canister to the ground!

"Why?!" Hawkeye asked, standing on a ledge above them. "Tell me the truth!"

But this was a part of Black Widow's plan. She was setting up Hawkeye! She wanted him to take the blame for the stolen Hulk sample!

Just then, a S.H.I.E.L.D. plane arrived. Black Widow pointed at Hawkeye. "Take him down!" she ordered. "He's a double agent working for HYDRA!"

Hawkeye was outnumbered. Soon, he had been captured.

"Take him to the vault," Black Widow ordered.

A short while later, Black Widow made a phone call.

"We'll need to arrange a new drop," she said. "But as far as S.H.I.E.L.D. is concerned, I just took down a traitorous double agent."

Then she held up the vial of the Hulk's DNA. **"Hail HYDRA . . ."**